LIES

AND OTHER TALL TALES

COLLECTED BY

ZORA NEALE HURSTON

ADAPTED AND ILLUSTRATED BY

CHRISTOPHER MYERS

HARPERCOLLINSPUBLISHERS

Sources as they appeared in *Every Tongue Got to Confess: Negro Folk-Tales from the Gulf States**:

Robert Bailey, middle age, worker in orange grove, barely literate, from
Georgia: pp. 20–21; Lonnie Barnes: p. 30; "Nigger" Henry Bird, about 25,
grove worker, born South Carolina: p. 38 ("That time a flea asked me");
George Harris, age 38, farmer, Alabama: p. 19; Arthur Hopkins, age 18,
schoolboy, but loads lumber at sawmill in summer, born in Florida
(reared in Alabama): pp. 6, 9, 14; N. A. James, about 40, YMCA secretary,
born in Louisiana: p. 34; David Leverett, age 19, sawmill hand, Alabama: p. 25;
Raymond McGill, about 35, works in phosphate mines, born in Florida: p. 27;
Edward Morris, age 15, eighth-grade education, born in Mobile, Alabama:
pp. 16, 37, 38 ("That wasn't cold at all"); Lorenzo Morris, age 18, high school,
born in Alabama: p. 24; Peter Noble, about 22, garage worker, North
Alabama: p. 28; Eugene Oliver, about 20 in 1928, about third-grade
education, sawmill hand: p. 10; Mae Oliver, sister to Eugene Oliver, about
22 in 1928, of about the same educational level as Eugene Oliver: p. 13;
Floyd Thomas, age 23, phosphate miner, born in Florida: p. 15; Joe Wiley:
p. 33; R. T. Williams, about 40, works in an orange grove, born in Georgia:
p. 31. *No source provided for text on p. 23

Library of Congress Cataloging-in-Publication Data is available.
ISBN 0-06-000655-2 — ISBN 0-06-000656-0 (lib. bdg.)
Typography by Carla Weise
2 3 4 5 6 7 8 9 10
❖
First Edition

To the keepers of culture—
all the writers and artists
who have influenced me
and been friends to me.
—C.M.

The Zora Neale Hurston Trust gratefully
thanks Christopher Myers for his superb
work. The Trust is also very thankful for
the vision and guidance of Susan Katz,
Kate Jackson, and our wonderful editor,
Phoebe Yeh. Lastly, our continued
appreciation of Cathy Hemming,
who initially brought us to HarperCollins
Children's Books, and Jane Friedman
and everyone at HarperCollins who works
tirelessly on behalf of Zora.

BACK IN THE DAY,

Way, way, back in the day,
Back when George Washington's hair on the one-dollar bill
  hadn't yet turned white.
Back when computers ran on steam power,
Back when cellular phones had rotary dials,
When they had to print the Internet in the newspapers,
When there was only two buttons on your remote control,
Back when a quarter was only worth a dime.
Back in those days,
There were lies,
Real lies,
Not "dog ate my homework" "bus was late" kind of lies.
Those lies aren't worth the hair on a flea's back.
Liars, back in the day, could tell a lie so good,
You didn't even want to know the truth.

SISTER ZORA

Zora Neale Hurston, who was studying anthropology
With a bunch of educational-type liars at Columbia University,
Came down south to talk to the professional liars she growed up with.
She wrote down lies upon lies.
'Cause she knew that there had been a decline
In the quality of lies and it was just
Gone get worse, unless somebody did something.
So she wrote down all the lies she could get her hands on.
She knew so many lies,
Every time she'd cough, a lie would slip out.
And if she sneezed, all the clocks in the room would tell
  the wrong time
'Cause they'd caught lying too.

These are some of the lies she collected.
I found them in a government office,
Which is where they are keeping all the lies nowadays

AND THAT'S THE TRUTH.

Once I seen
a man **so ugly,**
they threw him
in Dog River
and they could
skim ugly
for six months.

You think **he** was ugly?

I seen a man **so ugly,** he can go behind a jimson weed and **hatch monkeys.**

What is the **tallest** man you ever seen?

The **tallest**

man I ever seen

could stand

knee deep

in hell

and shake hands

with Gabriel.

Hmmm, that's tall.

What's the **biggest** man you ever seen?

That drives over me.

I know a man

so **big**

that when he went to

whip his boy, the boy

runned under his

stomach and stayed

hid under there

six months.

Well, I didn't know any man **that big.** But I seen a man **so short** he had to get up on a box to look over a grain of sand.

in a storm and never got wet

because she stepped

between the drops

That's a **little** woman. Woman like that leave a man hungry, cooking with them little pots. Reminds me of a man I know who was **so hungry** that he salted and peppered himself and **swallowed himself** and left nothing but his shadow.

That reminds me
of this one man.
He was **so mean**,
he greased another man
and **swallowed**
him whole.

You need to run fast
from a man like that.

I seen a man run

so hard that he

You need to be some kinda **smart** to know how that happened. But I knowed a man **so smart**, he had the seven-year itch and scratched it out in **three months**.

He was
dark-skinnded too.

That man was
so black
till he could
spit ink.

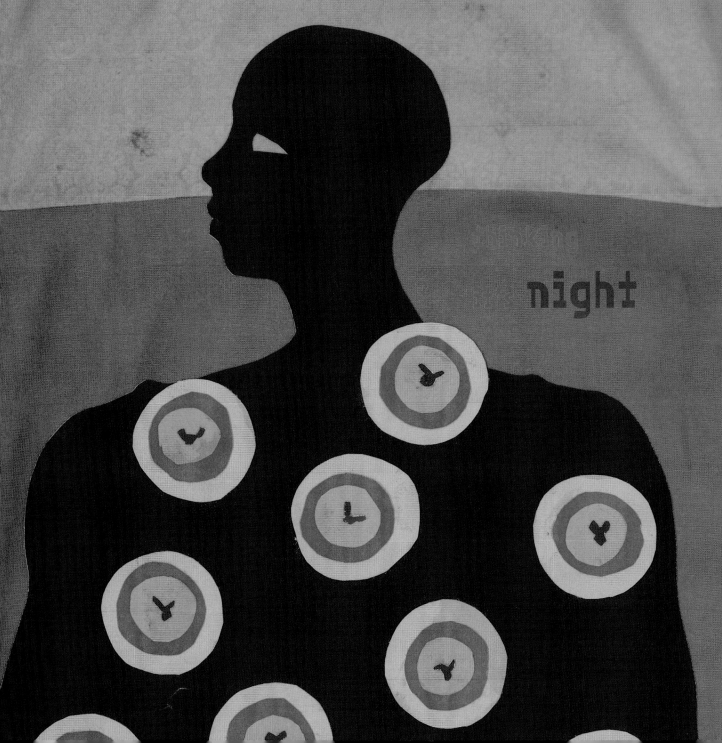

One time when it **was** night,
I was lost in the woods,
and I was lost **teetotally**.

I heard a racket over in the thicket.
I looked behind a log. It was the
moon changin'!

That's a strange sight to see. A man I know, he went hunting and saw **three thousand** ducks in a pond. Just as he leveled his gun to fire, the weather turned cool and the water in the lake froze solid, and them ducks flew off with the lake **froze to their feet**.

The weather do make for some strange sights, I agree. Like once, I seen it **so dry**, the fish came swimming up the road **in dust**.

When the earth is dry like that, you can't grow nothing. Ole Mitchell field was the poorest land I ever seed.

They built a church on it— had to use ten sacks Commercinal to fertilize de ground befo' they could raise a hymn on it.

I don't have **that** problem.

I have ground **so rich** until one day my father's mule died and he buried him out in the field. The next morning, guess what happened? The mule had **sprouted little jackasses**.

You is sho' nuff strowin' it.

But I believe you,
'cause I seen some
unbelievable
things in my day. Once
I seen wind **so hard**
till it blowed a man's
nose **off** his face and
onto the back of his neck,
and if he got a cold,
every time he sneeze,
**he blow
his hat off.**

Speaking of the cold,
I have known it to get
so cold, the words
all froze up and
fell to the floor like hail.
You would have to carry
a bucket along so when
someone talked to you,
you would put the words
in the bucket and carry
them home and put the
bucket on the stove and
let the words **melt**.

That wasn't cold at all. I seen it so cold till the fire was goin' somewhere to get warm. Even the sun was froze and the ice just melted today.

That time a flea asked me for a shoeshine—so I left.

Artist's Note

ZORA NEALE HURSTON met herself walking along a street in Port-au-Prince in Haiti. She knew she was herself because she looked just like herself, except maybe she was a little more country, or a little more city, or a little more something she couldn't put her finger on. Either way she struck up a conversation, because if you can't talk to yourself, who can you talk to?

"Girl" (she called herself "girl" because she liked herself), "girl, how do you find yourself such a long way from Eatonville?"

"I'm in Eatonville right now, sister," she replied.

"Oh . . ." She paused, puzzled. "Are you anywhere else?"

"I'm about fifteen places right now, which is a light day for me, which is why I even have time to have this conversation. I'm in Eatonville, talking to the folks, I'm at Columbia studying anthropology with Franz Boas, I'm driving down the highway laughing with Langston about our play, I'm asking people on 125th Street if I can measure their heads (how I ended up agreeing to do that I do not rightly know), I'm filming dancers in the Bahamas, I'm writing a script in Hollywood, where I work for Paramount Pictures, I'm in a phosphate mine, I'm singing onstage in Nashville."

"Well, thank you for taking the time out to talk to me. You have got to be the busiest woman I have ever seen." Zora was impressed.

"That we are, girl. That we are." Zora smiled and walked on, because she had places to be, and the other Zora did too.

There are so many Zora Neale Hurstons. She lived more lives in her time than she had room for. She was scientific and sympathetic, too social and too alone, a recorder of history, and a forward-thinking radical. She was rooted in all of her endeavors by a desire to tell stories, and an understanding that stories were at the center of the human experience.

This book is like Zora Neale. It has had a lot of lives, and I have tried to add a few more. The text has been adapted from some of Zora's anthropological writing, in which she collected these tall tales, which were used in some version of playing the dozens. Playing the dozens is an African-American cultural practice, which if you haven't heard about it, you better ask your mama! It includes mama jokes and humorous dissing, which if you don't know what dissing is, you don't have the sense God gave a flea.

Surely some of these inventive turns of phrase and wild stories had been around long before the people who told them to Zora, and if you hang out on street corners, at hair salons and the right kinds of eating establishments, you will hear these and many more tall tales repeated, updated, and created. I recommend M&G's Soul Food on 125th Street in Harlem, as a particularly fertile ground for language hounds; also the macaroni and cheese there is good.

The illustrations are made from scraps of fabric and pieces of paper—found materials I have tried to transform into "quilts" as witty and beautiful as the phrases Zora Neale Hurston found and, in recording them, transformed into lasting testaments to our vibrant and living African-American culture.